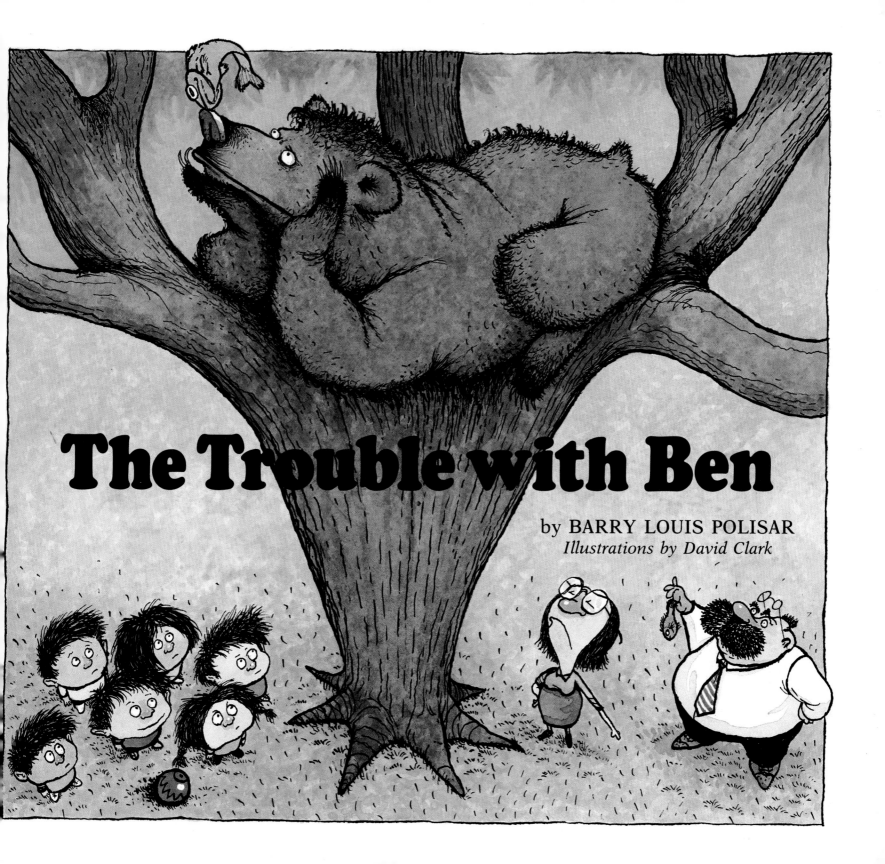

The Trouble with Ben

by BARRY LOUIS POLISAR

Illustrations by David Clark

Ben was different. And the other children knew it. Some of them wouldn't play with him and called him names. They said he was big and clumsy. They said he was weird.

Ben *was* bigger than most of the children in his school and he was a little clumsy. But he wasn't really weird.

He liked to run around the school yard and make funny yowling sounds. He loved to climb trees and swat at insects that buzzed around him. And when he ran, he'd get down on all fours and bound across the playground.

But that wasn't really weird to Ben. He enjoyed playing like that.

There were a lot of things Ben enjoyed doing.

He loved to jump through a hoop and ride a unicycle blindfolded. He could balance a fish on his nose—and even walk a tightrope.

And no one could dance like he could.

But Ben was always getting into trouble.

He had a hard time waking up in the morning, especially during the long, cold winter months. Sometimes he would miss the school bus and other times he'd fall asleep at his desk—right in the middle of class!

His teacher would scold him in front of everybody—and sometimes she'd send him to the principal's office.

Ben hated going to the principal's office.

The principal was a tall man with thick, dark eyebrows and a big, bushy moustache that made him look like a walrus.

He would look at Ben and say, "Benjamin, do you know why you were sent here today?"

Ben would look down at the ground, turn his head and say, "Harumphh!"

"Benjamin," he'd ask, "What is the matter with you? Why can't you behave like everyone else?"

"Harumphh," Ben would say.

Poor Benjamin. He never knew what to say.

He tried to be like everyone else, but things kept going wrong.

If the other kids in his class lined up to get a drink of water, Ben would try to drink too, but water would splash on everyone.

Some kids would giggle and some would get wet and start to cry. His teacher would rush out and Ben would be sent down to the principal's office—again.

Then the principal would raise his thick, bushy eyebrows, take off his glasses, shake his head, and sigh.

At home, his parents asked him the same questions the principal asked.

"Benjamin," his father demanded, "Why are you always getting into trouble? Why can't you be like everyone else?"

"Oh Benjamin," his mother would say. "I just don't know what we're going to do about you. If only you could learn to fit in."

"What's wrong with me?" Ben wondered.

Maybe his parents were right; if he were more like everyone else, things might be better.

He tried to dress like the other children. He even tried to eat like them. Nothing worked.

He wasn't like them. And trying to be just made him more unhappy. Ben was different, just like everyone said.

One day at school Ben was told to report to the office. When he got there, a man in a dark gray suit began to ask him questions.

"Ben," he asked, "Why do you insist on being different?" "Harumphh," Ben answered.

"Are you trying to get attention by acting this way?" the man continued. "Harumphh," Ben said again.

After a while, the man took off his glasses.

He rubbed his eyes and said, "Ben, there is no reason for you not to behave like other children."

"I want you to go outside and play with them," the man continued. "If you do what they do, you will learn how to fit in."

Ben ran outside. He hated running in clothes and felt funny in them. But he couldn't wait to get outside.

Everyone on the playground was screaming and shrieking. Some children were playing on the sliding board. Ben tried going down the slide, but he kept getting stuck.

Laura, the girl who sat next to him in class, was on the swings. Ben decided to swing also, but when he sat down, the swing broke. One of the boys ran to get the teacher.

"I'm in trouble now," he thought. Mrs. Traynor would send him to the principal for sure and the principal would call his parents again. He knew he would be punished.

But it wasn't his teacher who came. It was Mrs. Schonbrunn, the fourth grade teacher from the room next door.

"Ben broke our swing," Laura volunteered. "He's always getting in trouble and he's always bothering us. You should send him to the principal—that's what Mrs. Traynor always does."

Ben scrunched up his nose and groaned. He was ready to go to the principal's office again.

Suddenly, something was itching him. He began to scratch under his arm.

Mrs. Schonbrunn looked at Ben as he picked an insect off his coat. "Benjamin," Mrs. Schonbrunn said, "Please pay attention!"

Ben looked up at her. He began straightening out his clothes. He realized he *hadn't* been paying attention.

He did his best to listen, but there, hanging down over the fence beside her, was a branch, loaded with bright red berries and green leaves.

Ben reached for the branch and began eating the berries and chewing the leaves.

Mrs. Schonbrunn smiled. She walked back to the other side of the playground and didn't say a word.

And she didn't send him to the principal!

That night, Ben looked at himself in the mirror. He stuck out his bottom jaw and gnashed his teeth. He had good, sharp teeth, he thought.

He looked at his ears, his eyes, his nose. He brushed his hair away from his face and stood by the sink for a long time.

Ben didn't understand why everybody thought he should be like other children. When he tried to be like them, it didn't feel right.

Before going to bed, he took off his clothes and hung them in the closet. He took off his shoes and put them away, too. He didn't need them anymore.

The next afternoon, during recess, Ben balanced a fish on his nose. Laura and her friends gathered around him and watched. They had never seen anyone do that before. When he finished, some of the children actually applauded.

Of course, Ben got in trouble for bringing a fish to school, but he didn't care. He decided he had been getting bad advice; he wasn't going to try to be like everyone else any more.

He *was* different and there was nothing wrong with that. In fact, he sort of liked being different.

Maybe, if he could concentrate on the things he was good at, he could find a way to stay out of trouble.

He knew there were things he could do better than anyone else.

No one else could balance a fish on his nose or ride a
unicycle. And no one could dance like he could.

There were other things that his parents, his teacher, the
principal—and even the man in the gray suit didn't
understand. But he knew them.

Ben felt sad that they didn't understand, but he was
happy to be himself again. And he felt good.

Thanks go to Lynn Luderer who gave me some wonderful suggestions and help with this manuscript, to Sheldon Biber, who read all the drafts of this book without growling too much, and, of course, to my wife Roni, who knows what it's like to live with a rebellious bear. When I was bogged down in earlier drafts, Roni suggested I change directions and write about things I know about.

B.L.P.

THE TROUBLE WITH BEN © 1992 by Barry Louis Polisar
Illustrations © 1992 by David Clark

Published by Rainbow Morning Music
2121 Fairland Road; Silver Spring, MD 20904

ISBN 0-938663-13-5

First Edition   Printed in the United States of America